BLACK PETER

BLACK PETER

Gwendolyn S. Patton

Contents

PROLOGUE

It was beginning to look way too damn much like Christmas.

General Allegre turned up his collar against the cold and shivered. It would only get colder, he mused, as the snowflakes melted against his forehead. The ships were taking people off Earth in a steady stream, the UN forces doing their best to keep the peace as the shuttles landed in fields, deserts, even the blasted heaths that used to be cities and villages. The clouds swirled overhead in a silent, brooding ballet, a final performance of Swan Lake for the fair globe of Terra, stricken down by her most virulent of lifeforms.

Allegre tried not to feel the weight of the snow within them upon his heart, but could not. It seemed to squeeze him, smaller and smaller as he looked upwards. Finally, unable to stand it, he looked away, and kicked through the small drift before him and stomped into the bunker.

"Lieutenant, give me a status report," Allegre growled in the semi-gloom of the bunker's chill interior. A young man, swaddled in non-regulation winter-gear, a pair of vid-goggles covering his face, slapped at a vertiboard a few times.

"The Eastern Seaboard is clear, General. The West Coast reports they've been clear for about twelve hours. The southern sectors say they will be clear within four hours maximum. But we have a problem in North Sector Four."

Allegre sighed. "Of course we do. Elaborate, Lieutenant."

"The shuttles keep freezing up before they can get them de-iced. They're having trouble getting them off the ground, Sir. Fargo reports they're managing to get them up only after spending inordinate amounts of laser energy on deicing. It's slowing things too much. At current rate, they will not be clear by the zero hour."

Allegre shook his head. "They must be clear. Failure is not acceptable. Tell them to get clear."

"Sir, they can't get clear. Their shuttles . . . "

Allegre took a step and pulled the goggles from the young man's face, threw them across the bunker. The tinkle of broken glass was lost in the shout of surprise as the General lifted the lieutenant from his seat by the front of his parka. "Lieutenant, I am not interested in excuses. We have managed to lift three hundred million, four hundred seventy four thousand, nine hundred and four persons from this United States into space in the past six years. We have less than twelve hours to get the remaining quarter million off, one hundred and seventeen thousand of whom are in North Sector Four. If they are not in space by then, they will never be, and they will freeze to death. I will not allow more Americans than have died in all of our wars combined become *popsicles* on my watch. Am I understood?" He dropped the young man into his seat. Allegre loomed over the lieutenant like a Colossus, his brow roiling like the gray, gray clouds that circled the globe. "You get on the Net and tell them to find a way. Get those shuttles *moving*." And then he was gone, a wall of stricken purpose out the door amidst the fluttering flakes.

"Yes, Sir," the lieutenant whispered.

Carl screamed in anger and pounded on the laser housing, damn near burning his hand on the hot metal. The fragging thing had packed up for the tenth time and shut itself off. He could already see the ice beginning to reform on the shuttle's skin, twenty minutes' work wasted. "It's no damn use," he screamed into his boom mike, "the lasers just can't take the strain!"

"They've got to!" Matilda yelled in his ear. "There's only a few thousand more people to go—just two more shuttle loads, and then we can go ourselves. Come on, Carl, think of something!"

The housing of the recalcitrant device ticked and pinged as the freezing air swirled around it. Carl's eyes roved around the old airport, over the huge bulk of the passenger shuttle, the old air terminal full of refugees waiting to load when it came back from the orbital station—and the ancient hangars.

"I have an idea, Mattie . . . " He slammed the lift-bar on the maintenance cart to full and shot across the field towards the old hangars, the near-gale winds buffeting him like a leaf. "It's illegal as hell, but who cares now?"

"Carl—what the hell are you doing? Where are you going at a time like this?"

"Trust me, Mattie. I think this may work."

The old aluminum of the hangar doors pulled apart like paper under the handler beams of the maintenance cart. A good thing, too—he never could have made them open on their tracks—what ice had not jammed solid, years of rust and filth had. He tapped override commands into the cart's computer, and some of the ancient lights in the old hangar flickered to life.

Three old jet aircraft sat in the hangar, their wing-tips removed, but largely intact. If only . . . Carl tapped more commands into the computer, gave a hiss as information scrolled on his screen. "Mattie, get a crew out here to this old hangar. This is going to work, but I can't do this alone."

"What's going to work?"

"The lasers won't put out enough heat fast enough to clear the shuttles of ice. But if we can jockey these old jets out onto the tarmac, and get their engines running, the exhaust *will*."

There was a long, long, pause. "Carl, that has to be the craziest idea I've ever heard. Do you know how long those things have been mothballed out there?"

"According to the airfield comp, they were last run about five years ago, when they were moved from another hangar. There's even a tank of fuel adjacent to this hangar with stabilizer in it, in case they needed to move them again."

"Why not just use lifter fields?"

"Aviators. Go figure. Never mind that, Mattie. Get me some mechs and get 'em out here *fast*. Every minute you waste talking to me is a quarter inch of ice we have to melt!"

He didn't wait for the mechs. He found the storage tank and hoses, and laid them out using the manipulators of the maintenance cart. He checked over the ancient jet as well as he could, while lights moved towards the hangar. A huge snowplow trundled up, a path snaking towards the passenger shuttle. Mechanics jumped off the plow and ran towards the hoses and the jets, started to clamber atop them.

"Let's get a move on!" he shouted to the lead mech, "Check the fuel tanks! Spray everything with quik-seal if you have to—the last thing we need is to blow ourselves up with a fuel leak."

Ten minutes later, the first jet's engines gave a strangled whine and coughed to life. It lurched on partially-flat tires as it trundled forward, the mechs jumping off to work on the next jet. The snowplow moved aside as the ancient aircraft wheeled out into the swirling snow, towards the waiting spacecraft. It had barely gotten a quarter of the way across the field when the second jet's nose poked from the hangar.

Carl jockeyed the first jet into place, swinging it in a 180-degree turn so the huge engines pointed towards the shuttle. "Brakes—on. Okay, stick the chocks under the wheels!" A maintenance cart slammed huge metal wedges under the tires, and manipulators grabbed hold of the aircraft's frame. "I sure hope this works," Carl whispered, as he increased the throttles.

Hot exhaust shrieked from the engines and sluiced over the ice-sheathed shuttle, the air shimmering in waves. The plane shuddered against the chocks, and manipulator fields glowed as it fought to move forward, but was held solidly in place. The second plane moved into position, and a minute later, hot jet wash from that craft joined the first.

A brilliant flash of light split the night, as the third ancient craft, halfway across the airfield, exploded in a fireball. "Dammit!" screamed Carl, as he watched helplessly from his own cockpit. "Who was in that plane?"

"Frank Mitchell was in it alone. He didn't like the looks of the fuel lines, even after three cannisters of Quik-Seal, so he wouldn't let anyone else go with him," said Mattie over his headset.

"Damn . . . " Carl nudged the throttles. "Is the ice melting? Is this working?"

"Yes! It's working!" screamed one of the mechs over the radio. "Better than the lasers, at least! The shuttle will be clear in just a couple of minutes!"

"Good, because we'll need to do this twice more," Carl said wearily. "Get ready to pull the chocks so we can move these things out of the way, so they can launch."

Five minutes later, the shuttle lifted off, ice cleared enough to navigate. Two hours later, the next shuttle lifted.

The final shuttle, with the ground crews and military personnel, would be just a little late.

Chapter 1

Carl was ready to go. The last shuttle was all loaded, the jets bellowing without pilots on the tarmac, jet washes keeping the ice from forming on the shuttle's composite hull. He was very glad he didn't have to pilot the shuttle. His work was finally done, and he could rest. He sighed, closed his eyes, and waited for the drive field to lurch them into motion.

His shuttle was the last . . . the last shipful of refugees from a dying Earth. The ancient jet airplanes he had resurrected would scream a banshee's keening as the world's last escaping sons and daughters tore themselves from the rapidly-freezing surface. The jihads had finally come, anger had turned into rocks falling from the sky, dust obscuring the sun, bringing bitter, bitter cold.

But now, Carl Merriweather, spacecraft mechanic, could finally sit back and rest.

"Don't be so sure that you can rest, Carl Merriweather," said a voice in his ear.

Carl's eyes flashed open. "Who said that?"

"Who said what, eh?" said Matilda Jones, sitting next to him. She was a short, somewhat-plump woman with frizzy reddish hair and a snub nose, a dash of freckles across her pale cheeks. "You hearing things, Carl?"

"I could have sworn someone just said something to me." He shook his head and looked around. There was no one else near that looked conscious. The other people in the seats near his were the other mechs from his team, most of whom were either asleep or nearly so.

There was a whine as the drive fields cycled, and the lights dimmed slightly. Everyone took a breath in anticipation. Then . . .

Nothing. The sound simply stopped, chopped off abruptly. The lights in the cabin flickered and winked out, plunging the cabin into darkness. Someone yelled, then there was pandemonium as everyone awoke to the sudden fact that the shuttle wasn't launching.

Carl felt a hand on his sleeve. "Come with me," said a voice. The hand tugged, hard. Carl released his seat-web and got up, following the person's lead. They went to the airlock and stepped into it. A single light burned in the panel, obscured for a moment as a hand covered it, pressed the cycle button. The inner door closed, the outer slid open.

Outside was a *sleigh*. It hovered just outside the shuttle doorway, unsupported. "Get in," said the voice. "Do it. I don't have time for explanations."

Carl got into the sleigh, which bobbed slightly under his weight. The other person got in beside him and pushed him down onto the padded bench. The stranger reached out and took a hold of what appeared to be simple leather reins and shook them sharply. "Okay, dash away then," he said crossly. The sleigh leaped away from the side of the shuttle . . . and into the sky.

Behind and below them, the shuttle lit up again. Moments later, the drive field glowed to life, and the shuttle lifted from the field and clawed for space.

Carl gripped the wooden railing of the sleigh and wondered if jet exhaust caused hallucinations. For in front of the sleigh he could swear he saw *reindeer*. Eight—no, nine reindeer, each galloping for all it was worth into the swirling gray clouds. A piercing ray of bright red light lanced ahead of the sleigh from the lead animal, and Carl shook his head. No, not possible. Definitely not possible.

He wasn't cold, for one thing. Here he was, sitting in an open sleigh in the sky flying through the coldest possible snowstorm in the world, and he wasn't even cold. No snowflakes were hitting him. He was actually warm, if you could credit it.

"Of course you're warm, idiot. Do you think I'd fly in this fool thing if I had to put up with the elements?" said his pilot.

Carl turned wild eyes on his pilot, half expecting, half fearing to see a jolly fat man in a red suit. He was not prepared to see a skinny black man in a grimy outfit that was half Arabian Nights, half Spanish Main, a sooty black coat of some European design—Carl could see German-looking eagles on the buttons—thrown over it, a worn top-hat on his head and a threadbare scarf about his neck.

"Who . . . what . . . ?" stammered Carl.

The black man rolled his eyes. "Well, you've obviously figured out that this is Kris's sleigh, or you wouldn't have been expecting to see him when you looked at me. Do you know any Christmas legends? Any history?" Seeing Carl's blank stare, he snorted. "Figures. No one remembers me. I guess it's a good thing, though." He raised a hand, encased in a fingerless glove, and tipped his hat briefly. "I, Sir, am Black Peter."

"Who?"

"Black Peter. *Schwartzer* Peter, the dark companion of Kris Kringle?" He searched Carl's face in the semi-gloom of the storm. "Gah. Never heard of me, have you? Well, Mr. Merriweather, old jelly belly didn't always work alone. He used to have a sidekick."

"Well, I knew he had elves . . . "

"They're just hired help. I was his *partner.*"

"What about Mrs. Claus?"

Black Peter growled something that might have been Spanish. "Feh. Beard of the Prophet, don't get me started on that cow. It's her fault we stopped working together. Prejudiced, she is."

"But, who *are* you?"

"Look, it's like this. Used to be, Kris gave out the goodies to the good kids, but he left the punishing of the bad kids to me. I was his enforcer. None of the kids up in our neck of the woods had ever seen a black man before, so I was REAL scary. Worked like a charm, let me tell you! One touch of ol' Black Peter's switch, and they behaved themselves all the next year."

"I thought Santa gave lumps of coal . . . "

"That was *her* idea. She didn't want him working with me, and had gotten some silly-ass idea in her head that giving the nasty little snots a good switchin' when they needed it somehow 'scarred their psyches' or some nonsense. Made me want to puke, let me tell you—hang on, we're gonna hit some turbulence for a few minutes." The sleigh bucked a bit as it went through a particularly nasty storm-front, and Carl fought with his stomach for dominance.

"So . . . Black Peter? What do you want *me* for?" Carl managed to stammer out.

"You're a maintenance mech, right?"

"Ah, yeah . . . "

"Well, we need a maintenance mech."

"Couldn't you just pick up a phone?"

"No. Had to be one that believed in Santa."

"But I don't!"

Peter gave Carl a look. "Oh, come on. Who was it that expected to see the fat man himself in this seat? Ever since you saw a sleigh outside the shuttle, you've been hoping for a look at Santa Claus. You never did believe that he didn't exist, even when everyone told you so, did you?"

"But, I don't get it. I thought Santa Claus was a myth." Carl let out a yip as the sleigh slewed around a tall, pointed mountaintop.

"He is. So am I. Now shut up, this bit is tricky." The sleigh started bucking and weaving so badly that Carl couldn't do anything except grip the sleigh and his stomach. Peter handed him a paper stomach-distress bag, which he used a bare moment later.

The sleigh rolled and dipped like a mad thing, reminding Carl of nothing less than a sparrow chasing a bug. He certainly felt as though he'd eaten a bug, and wished he had more of the stomach-distress bags—the one Peter had given him was distressingly full. He was afraid to simply lean over the side, for fear the slipstream would rip him free. He wasn't sure the force field, or whatever it was that kept the snow from pelting him in the face, extended to vomit, anyway. He turned a clamped jaw and pained eyes to the grinning Peter, who silently handed him a few more of the bags.

"Get any of that muck on me, and I'll beat the crap out of you," he yelled over the howl of the wind, snapping the reins wildly. "Kris may put up with kids puking on his lap, but I never did tolerate it!" Carl nodded miserably and heaved into another bag. "Go ahead and toss the full ones over the side. The only thing you'll hit now is icebergs."

Carl heaved the full bags over the side, where they whirled away in an instant. Watching them proved to be a mistake, and he filled yet another one. It joined the first two on the winds.

The sleigh's rollicking ride suddenly smoothed, and they broke out into clear air—and Carl gasped. Below them was a city. It sprawled like a vast snowflake of concrete and steel, ablaze with lights of all colors.

A blazing green lance of light seared past them, and Peter swore like a longshoreman, slewing them to the side. "Dammit, who did that?" He flipped open a panel to reveal a very ordinary looking radio set, grabbed a hand mike. "Hey, lay off the laser fire! It's Black Pete!"

There was no reply on the radio except staticky pops and crackles, but there were no more laser blasts, either. Pete circled the city once and angled towards a large, gaping tunnel in the side of a low, flat building. The reindeer snorted and seemed almost to backpedal, slowing the sleigh like a small airplane stalling in for a landing. At the last moment, large doors snapped to the side, showing a brightly-lit interior. The hooves of the reindeer sparked as they touched the surface, then the runners of the sleigh scraped with a screech.

Chapter 2

Carl noticed that his hands hurt. They were clenched on the wooden railing before him, a wad of empty stomach-distress bags crushed between them. He breathed a sigh of relief that the bags had in fact been empty, and pried his hands loose, flexing them to get some feeling back into them. Then his ears were being assaulted by the loudest and most vituperous stream of invective he had ever been unfortunate enough to witness—all in languages he did not know, as both Black Peter and a short, stocky man in an insulated jumpsuit started screaming at each other.

Pete seemed to be using some obscure Spanish dialect, interspersed with Arabic, while the short fellow seemed to be cursing in some form of Gaelic or Celtic. Pete didn't show any conciliatory signs, standing directly over the short man and waving his arms madly, screaming at the top of his lungs. Then the short man took off his padded helmet and whacked Pete in the crotch with it, hard.

Pete let out a great *whoosh* and sat down on the cold, hard surface of the landing strip and let out a strangled screech, curling around his pelvis for an agonized moment, then his hands curled forward into talons, reaching for the short man's neck. But the little man was already balling up his fists and stepping forward.

"Enough!" bellowed a voice from above, as a long, feathered arrow slammed into the floor between them. Pete backed up very rapidly,

seeming to walk using his buttocks, a very strange form of locomotion, but understandable, seeing as the arrow had embedded itself in concrete only a handspan or so from his manhood. The short, stocky little man jumped back with a yell and craned his neck upwards, running a hand through his hair to get it out of his eyes. Carl looked upward, too, to see where he was looking.

There was another little man hovering overhead. A little man with wings. A little man with wings in camouflage gear. A little man with wings in camouflage gear with a very nasty-looking compound bow. They weren't bird wings. They were lacy, gossamer *fairy* wings, beating very rapidly in the chill air. His face was very stern, and his bow was pulled back and a very nasty looking arrow already placed on the string.

Black Pete climbed laboriously to his feet, holding his crotch. "Cupid, you *ebn el metanaka*, you almost hit me in the nuts with that thing!"

"Not a chance, you Moorish sadist. I *hit* what I aim at. As the Great Nuge hath said: *'Nature heals and the Hunt fuels the soul'*. You two should be ashamed of yourselves. Noggin, this does not become you, especially." The flying man lowered his bow, but did not return the arrow to his quiver.

The little man growled. "He stole the Boss's sleigh. Could have killed all my babies!" He shot Pete a dark look. "Damn sadist!"

"Hey, now!" I never hurt an animal in my life!" complained Pete.

"So you say! What about the Missus' cat?"

"The damned beast scratched me!"

"But *shellac?*" And the two lapsed into foreign language again, screaming and spitting.

The little man in camo came in for a landing next to Carl. "Sorry about them. I assume you're the spaceship mech?" Carl nodded.

"Carl, Carl Merriweather. Ummm . . . I'm starting to feel a little . . . well . . . "

"Freaked?" said the little man, putting the arrow in his quiver and slinging the bow over his shoulder. "Well, I don't much blame you." He stuck out a hand. "I'm Cupid. Nice to meetcha." Carl took it, feeling like a grownup shaking a ten-year-old's hand. "Good handshake, nice and solid. As the Great Nuge doth say, *Fight for what you believe in. Rock like ya mean it.*"

"Nuge?"

"Ted Nugent. Man was like a god to me. C'mon, I'll take you to the Boss."

Something went *ping* in Carl's brain. "Hang on. You're *Cupid?* As in the cherub that . . . "

"Yeah, yeah. Shoots the arrows of love. Yup, ya got me, champ. But Nugent taught me the REAL way. Hunting. As the Great Nuge doth say: *'Hunting will wake up the beast within. You will rock harder. You will live bigger. You will love more intensely. You will soar with eagles on high!! I promise you this.'* The Nuge has never steered this cherub wrong, Bloodbrother!" Cupid whacked Carl companionably on the back and led the way across the huge hangar.

Carl rubbed his shoulder—a companionable whack from the cherub felt like being pelted with a sling-shot.

Pete and the little man, Noggin, continued to scream at one another, while reindeer watched with bored expressions. It didn't occur to Carl until they were leaving the hangar that Noggin's ears had come to distinct, delicate points.

Chapter 3

Carl and Cupid walked down a very ordinary-seeming corridor, the floor a very normal looking green linoleum with little speckles in it. Carl half expected the air to be cold, but it wasn't. It was a very comfortable temperature. He didn't need his parka zipped up, so he unzipped it.

Cupid didn't so much walk as flutter, taking a few steps, buzzing into the air for a few yards, then lighting again on the floor for a few more dancing steps. His bow jiggled above his shoulder, and his quiver over the other. He certainly didn't look much like a cherubic bringer of love—more like a cherubic bringer of dinner.

They traveled like this for a few minutes until they came to a large atrium, which bustled with activity and light. In the center of the atrium was a sight that staggered even Carl's saturated synapses.

It was a starship.

Most starships were huge, ungainly affairs that could never touch the surface of a planet. They weren't economical to build small enough to land on a world—unless one didn't care about such things as economy and money and sheer scale. The subquantum drive used by starships was not particularly complex, but it was sensitive to gravitational effects, and it was much easier to build a stardrive that did not have to deal with a planet's heavy gravity field. But here sat a ship that was designed for both interstellar travel and planetary landing capability. It was immense, clearly capable of holding thousands of persons or huge volumes of cargo, and it sat seemingly ready to launch into the sky. Carl craned his neck and looked above to the huge dome, with massive motors standing ready to open, to allow the massive vessel to launch. Small forms crawled and climbed all over the ship, with ladders and lines and portable catwalks, tiny forms stuffed headfirst into inspection hatches and open panels, the bright lights of electrical arcs flashing dangerously within.

Carl looked at this behemoth and forgot for a moment to breathe.

"A beaut, ain't she?" said Cupid.

Carl could only nod.

"Too bad she's broken," said the cherub.

Carl started breathing with a whoosh and turned to face the little man. "Broken?"

"Yup. We've tried twice now to launch, and she won't budge. The crew's gone over every circuit, every nut, every bolt, every single blessed chip and wire. But they can't find anything wrong."

"So why doesn't it fly?"

Cupid looked worried. "That's why you're here. C'mon. They're waiting."

They walked around the perimeter of the starship until they reached a glass-walled office. Cupid pushed open the door, and they stepped inside. Two people sat at a large conference table, one slender, white-haired woman, one very rotund white-haired man. The woman looked up from her papers and frowned.

"I thought I vetoed this project, Cupid," she said, a dangerous note in her voice.

"Uh . . . " said the cherub.

"Now, Britt," rumbled the large man. "It isn't his fault."

"Kris, you know how I feel about having my orders ignored!" She stood and leaned on the edge of the table. "I told that *schvartzer* that we didn't *need* an outsider! So what is he doing here?"

"Hey, now," started Carl, starting to feel more than a little put out.

"You keep out of this," the woman said. "Where is that black troublemaker, anyway? Peter! Where are you? Get your lazy, sadistic black ass . . . " The woman strode out of the room, slamming the glass door dangerously wide in her wake. The fat man looked pained and puffed a little, mopped his brow with a handkerchief.

"I'm sorry about my wife, fellow," he said. "She's on a bit of a tear, given the circumstances and all." He levered himself from his chair with a grunt and waddled over, stuck out a huge hand. Carl shook it. It felt like shaking an inflatable swimming pool. "I'm Kris, Kris Kringle. I'm the owner hereabouts, though Britt—that's my wife, you met her, sort of—she's actually CEO and Chief of Operations. What did you say your name was?" He plumphed back down in his chair and looked as if his heart was about to give out any moment from the strain.

"Carl Merriweather. Um. So. Uh. You're Santa Claus?"

The big man nodded sadly. "Yes, 'fraid so, Son. Hey, are you all right?"

Carl's vision was flickering a bit. "Am I all right?" He leaned on the back of a chair and swayed. "Am I *all right?*" He wiped a hand across his forehead, which came away glistening with sweat. "No, I'm not all right! An hour ago, I was on the last shuttle off Earth from North America, bound for a starship for the colony where I'm supposed to be making my new life. Then I'm taken off the ship by a weird black man who says he's a *myth* on a flying sleigh pulled by reindeer, we nearly get fried by lasers, yelled at by an elf, shot at by a cherubic Ted Nugent fan, and now I'm called names by Mrs. Claus, and you ask me if I'm *all right?*"

Kris Kringle looked at him quizzically. "Well, are you?"

Carl rolled his eyes. "I've been better." And put his head in his hands.

There was a long, long silence.

"Would you like some eggnog?" said Kris.

Another silence.

"Sure," said Carl.

The fat man passed Carl a cupful of frothy yellow liquid. Carl sipped at it delicately. It was delicious.

A moment later, it nearly cooked in the cup as the air blistered around him. Mrs. Claus and Black Peter came charging into the room, voices raised to the breaking point. Mrs. Claus was yammering in some Norwegian-sounding dialect, while Peter had lapsed once again into a Spanish/Arabic mixture that sounded downright illegal. Finally, Mrs. Claus paused to take a breath, and Peter pounced on the momentary silence.

"Kris, tell her it wouldn't hurt to let Carl take a *look!*"

There was sudden silence.

All eyes turned on Kris, who sat and seemed to melt under the gaze of five sets of eyes.

Cupid broke the silence. "I'm outta here. I'm beginning to feel like a moth in a real big bug-zapper," and flitted out the door.

Kris grimaced and clutched at his chest, wheezing.

"Now see what you've done, you sadist!" screeched Mrs. Claus, leaping to her husband's side.

"Oh, he's fine—he just doesn't want to answer!" said Pete. "Quit it, you old fraud!"

Kris just moaned and closed his eyes.

"Get out of here!" screamed Mrs. Claus. "And take your grease monkey with you! We'll discuss this later!"

"Fine, fine, whatever . . . *takool zep ala hamada, pendeja puta* . . ." he started muttering. Carl recognized the Spanish part, knew it was obscene, but the rest had to be something Moorish. He took Carl's arm. "C'mon, Slick. Let's get you someplace you can rest."

Carl didn't argue. He let Pete lead him out of the room, while Mrs. Claus fluttered over the moaning Kris Kringle.

Pete took Carl into a side corridor, and into what appeared to be a small apartment. "This one's vacant. I reserved it for you this morning." Carl goggled to see a perfectly ordinary household catering terminal on one wall, which Pete stepped up to. "Hungry? Thirsty?" Carl nodded dumbly. "Bet you are. Here, I'll order some stuff." He punched buttons. A few moments later, a "ding" announced the tray in the dumbwaiter. He removed the tray, and tempting odors assailed Carl's nose. "Hope you like macaroni and cheese. Got that and some roast beef. And some tea." He set out plates, poured tea from an insulated pot.

Carl looked at the thoroughly-prosaic food and just shook his head. "This is too damned much," he whispered. "I'm at the North Pole, visiting Santa Claus and all his buddies, getting yelled at by Mrs. Claus. And I'm eating mac and cheese."

Pete sat down on the opposite side of the table. "Hey, it's understandable. This is a crazy situation. If we weren't so desperate, we wouldn't even have brought you into it, not like this."

Carl stabbed a fork into his macaroni. "Why do you need a starship, anyway? Aren't you all just a bunch of collective unconscious or something? You said you were a myth."

Pete took a sip of tea. "It's a strange situation. Yeah, we're mythical, every one of us, but we have an objective reality too. Each of us sprang from some original Prime Mover, and have evolved from there as the myth surrounding us has evolved. And somewhere, somehow, we achieved enough solidity that we need a spacecraft in order to leave Earth." He set his cup down, and it clicked with a solid finality. "We don't know how it happened, precisely, but it did."

Carl munched his food. It tasted good. The macaroni and cheese was the best kind, the kind that was baked in a large pan until the top got all brown and crunchy. The tea was strong, hot, and sweet, just how he liked it. "Well, I'm here now. Tell me what's going on. We seem to have time."

Pete nodded, and took a bite of beef. "What do you know of the origins of Santa Claus?"

"Not much. What any kid knows. He knows if you're naughty or nice, he brings toys to the good kids, a lump of coal to the naughty kids. He comes down the chimney, leaves the presents, does it all in one night. He lives up here at the North Pole, and elves make the toys and stuff."

"Well, that's the current version. It wasn't always like that.

"A long time ago, back in Norway, and later, in Germany, there was a young man named Kris Kringle—or a name to that effect—who would bring gifts at the Yule festival to the children in the villages in his region. At one point, he acquired a sidekick, a Spanish Moor called Black Pete . . .

"Like Robin Hood and his Moorish friend . . . "

"Yeah, very much like that. During the time before the Crusades, there was an awful lot of travel back and forth between our lands, for one thing or another. Some of us made friends and stayed, disparity of faith notwithstanding. I was one of those.

"Well, while Kris gave out the goodies, he never was any good at meting out any kind of punishment. He's basically a softy, and couldn't hurt a child to save his life. So he left that to me. I'd give the bad kids a good switching, and they'd never forget it. It was just the way we were raised. We were both very giving men. He liked to give presents and joy, and I liked to give the discipline of an ordered adulthood, like my father gave to me. I'm not a sadist, like that infidel *houri* keeps calling me."

"How did you know who was naughty and nice? Magic?"

"Hardly. Everyone knew everyone back then. The parents simply told us. But they told the kids that we knew by magic. It made it that much more powerful for the little brats. Like I told you before, they never saw anyone like me before, so I scared the living pee-waddins out of 'em. Once they got a switching from Black Peter, they never wanted another one, let me tell you!

"There were old magics back in those days, Carl, ancient and powerful. They liked what we were doing, and when we passed on from old age, we . . . didn't. We kept on going. Or something of us did. The idea of us, made solid, made real, if you will. It let us go farther, do more. We could cover more ground, do it faster. We actually could tell if the tykes were naughty or nice, and things were *good*." He took a bite of macaroni and seemed to brood.

"Then things changed. He met *her*."

"Mrs. Claus?"

"Britt Vargsdottir. I grant, she was a cutie back then, and I don't blame him for getting a raging stiffo over her, but he lost it big time. And that changed everything."

Carl was entranced. "How? What did it change?"

"Well, you see, Britt's a Christian."

"That changed things?"

"Of course it did! Didn't you hear me? We used to bring *Yule* gifts. Britt didn't approve of Kris celebrating Pagan holidays!" He punctuated his words with a forkful of beef. "It gets worse. She wasn't all that pleased that he was hanging out with me, either. She's a tad bigoted. Both because I'm Moorish and because I'm an infidel."

"A what?"

"What religion do you think a Spanish Moor would be, bucko?"

"I dunno."

"I'm a Muslim."

"Ah. I can see why she'd be annoyed."

"Especially around the time of the Crusades."

"Ah."

"Betcher ass. And she seemed to have some kind of sick idea that there was something—else—going on between me and Kris." His eyes clouded. "Sick bitch."

"You mean she thought you were . . . "

"Don't say it or I'll break your face," Pete said.

"Not a word."

"Good man. Like I was saying, she didn't like it one bit that Kris was bringing Pagan gifts, so she decided to make him over."

Carl didn't like the sound of that. "I smell something nasty."

"Ooh, you betcha. She decided to . . . appropriate . . . Christmas."

Chapter 4

Carl felt vaguely sick at the sound of that word. "Appropriate?"

"You never wondered why Santa got associated with Christmas? Best they can figure, Christ was born in the Spring, not December."

Carl thought about it. "I always thought it was something the ad agencies thought up."

Pete thumped the table. "Exactly!"

"Exactly?"

"Britt started an ad campaign to associate Kris with Christmas. She got this great idea to start what she called a secular-non-secular schism in the holiday, and to jam the two stories together. And it *worked*.

"People started to associate Christmas with both Christ and Kris—Christ for the religious aspects, and Kris for presents. I tried to argue with her that the meaning behind the gifts was gone, because they weren't for Yule anymore, but she wouldn't listen. She just drew parallels to the gifts of the Wise Men or some such and shut me off. The Church loved it, because they were trying to kill off the Pagan holidays themselves. This just fit right in with their plans."

Carl's eyes lit up. "What about Saint . . . "

Pete's eyes widened with alarm. "Don't! Please, if you ever want to stay in Kris's good graces, don't bring that one up. He really gets pissed when someone brings up that parallel. That was the one mistake Britt made, making a connection between Kris and Nicholas of Myra. Kris really hates that one. He never could see any real comparison between himself and that guy. Unfortunately, it was one of the most successful of the parallels in much of Europe."

"So where are things now?"

"Well, Britt didn't stop there. She went whole hog with the North Pole thing, and started pushing Kris harder and harder. The sleigh was her idea, and the reindeer. Put a bug in the ear of some artist, I imagine. The lump of coal was Kris's sop to working without me. He won't actually punish a child, the worst he'll do is disappoint one, and even then, he'd give something that might conceivably be of value to the parents, if only to cook the Christmas meal.

"Then she started on other holidays."

Carl looked aghast. "You don't mean . . . "

"Yup. Cupid. Valentine's day. Saint Valentine and Cupid. She's working on Saint Patrick and a bunch of leprechauns. And just wait until you meet the Easter Bunny."

"She messed with the Easter Bunny?"

"Messed with him? Heck, she created him! Easter had no non-secular component at all before she started mucking about. She took a harmless little bunny and started him rolling eggs around! Why eggs, for goodness' sake? Why not an Easter chicken? No, she had to have a bunny. Now the poor thing is schizo from the dichotomy between the religious and commercial aspects of the holiday. It's sad, really."

"Sad? This is insane!"

"Yeah, and she pays for it all by siphoning off money from all the Christian nations of the world."

Carl put down his fork. "She does what?"

"She's had her fingers in the international banking system for centuries. All the countries that have Christmas contribute a portion of their National product to the North Pole Operation, totally without their knowledge, of course. Where do you think the resources to do all this stuff comes from?"

"But an operation of this magnitude—it's unbelievable."

"It is that. And now we're all gonna freeze to death unless you can get that blasted starship off the ground." He finished his tea. "Why don't you try to take a nap. I'm going to see if I can't get the Missus to listen to reason."

Carl tried to sleep on the room's small bed, but he kept tossing and turning. The bed wasn't designed for a man of his size, so some part of his body was constantly hanging over the edge, and that part would get cold. The chill would penetrate his subconscious and remind him that, in perhaps two or three days at the most, life would become impossible on Earth, even with artificial power.

He'd wake up with a start, wondering what the hell had happened to his apartment decor. It would take him a few minutes to fall asleep again, to dreams of screaming elves and Ted Nugent riding a reindeer in a blizzard . . . and the cycle would repeat.

Then, he awoke to a pair of pink, bloodshot eyes only a few inches from his own.

"Gahhhh!" he screeched, rolling to the side. A whimpering cry came from the direction of the eyes, and Carl heard a fuzzy thump hit the floor. He peeked over the edge of the bed and saw a white, furry form quivering on the carpet.

"Please, don't hit me," piped a muffled voice from beneath the furry lump. "Just don't let them get me!"

Carl had to repress the urge to say *awww* . . . "I won't hurt you," he said softly. "Who is out to get you?"

"The Swiss Guard—they're *everywhere!*"

Carl had to think. "You mean the Vatican Police?"

"*Where? Where?*" The shape squirmed frantically.

It was a *rabbit*.

"No, no! There's no one here but us!"

The rabbit was babbling. "You have to get me off this planet, Mister Man—please—if you don't, they'll get me, and they'll do such terrible things to me!"

"Well, I'll do what I can, of course, but . . . "

The diminutive shape on the floor seemed to expand suddenly. "'But'?" it said. The voice was no longer soft and pleading. "There is no 'but', Mister Man. You do not know what they're like. I will not let them get me! Not again!" The rabbit was huge, standing on his hind legs, eyes blazing and teeth gleaming.

"Hey, now..."

"Fail me at your peril, Mister Man!" screeched the monstrous rabbit-thing. Then it whirled, shrinking rapidly, and vanished into a ventilator with a broken grill.

Carl ran out the door, shouting for Pete at the top of his lungs. Only a few moments later, the lanky Moor came barreling down the corridor, to witness Carl being calmed by a mixed bag of elves.

"What's up? Bad dream?" he said,as he shoved through the crowd.

"R . . . R . . . Rab . . . Rabb . . . " Carl stammered, pointing at his room. Pete's eyes widened, and he dashed into the room. He sniffed, then bent and examined the vent.

"Awww, *crap*!" he yelled, jumping to the terminal. He slapped a code. "Cupe? The furry nutball got *loose*! Yes, I'm sure, you flutterbrain! He just scared the crap out of Carl, that's how I know!" There was an exasperated sound from the terminal. "How should I know? You're the disciple of the Great Nuge! Find the damned lunatic before he kills someone!" He slammed the disconnect, walked back into the hall.

Chapter 5

"That was the *Easter Bunny*?" Carl whined, as Peter led him down the corridor.

"'Fraid so," he said. "He used to be fairly lucid. But he's gotten . . . irrational in the past few decades."

Carl shook his head. "This is too weird. That thing . . . changed. Looked like some kind of demon."

Pete nodded. "He does that. He used to be just a cute little bunny, back when he was just a pagan fertility symbol. Britt and her damned ad campaigns, though. She drove him nuts, Christianizing him. That creature you saw is what the Dutch call *Krampus*, the fertility demon. Supposedly, St. Nicholas keeps Krampus in chains and forces him to give treats to kids. That was Britt, trying to replace me in Kris's legend. Didn't work, though."

"He said something about the Swiss Guard."

"The Pope's personal guard, yeah. Sometime in the 1970s, he got real weird, and started to think the Catholics were out to get him."

"Were they?"

Pete shrugged. "The Church complained about the non-secular nature of the Easter Bunny, saying he had nothing to do with Jesus and Easter." They stopped in the middle of the corridor. "Damn rabbit got paranoid, thought the Church was after him. The last straw was when he tried to ask a U. S. President for political asylum."

Carl's eyes got wide "Don't tell me it was Jimmy Carter!"

Pete grinned. "You win the shiny new dime quiz, L'il Tommy. It was April 20th, 1979. Mr. Peanut is fishing peacefully. Then this rabbit swims up and starts talking. Mr. Peanut screams for the Secret Service, and Nutburger here does a Neanderthal Rabbit meets Jaws act and tries to eat the President's canoe." He sighed. "Cupid and I locked him up after that, but he keeps chewing his way out." He shook his head.

"He's convinced he has to get offworld to escape the Pope," said Carl.

Pete looked sour. "Vatican City was evacuated twenty months ago. Pope's on his way to Nova Roma by now. The idiot thinks it's a trick." He grabbed Carl's arm. "If we don't get the ship working, we won't be leaving at all. C'mon."

He led the way back to the atrium, the massive bulk of the starship looming overhead. It swarmed with diminutive figures in jumpsuits, crawling in and out of hatches and open panels. Peter didn't stop to talk to anyone, he just led Carl by the arm into an open airlock near the stern of the great craft. Carl shuddered to see both doors of the airlock open, something you almost never saw, a clear sign that something was dreadfully wrong with the ship—that was only done when a ship was incapable of going to vacuum. The corridors of the ship were much like any other starship, but with subtle differences that only a mech would notice. Aesthetically, the ship was a work of art. Technically, it was a mishmash of stock items from the larger hyperspace manufacturers, Tachytech, HyperMech, ArianeSpace-Martin-Marietta. The mixture of technologies was amazing.

"I always wished I could have built a ship like this," Carl murmured.

"Oh?" Pete said, leading him through a hatchway. "Like it, do you?"

"It's amazing! HyperMech integrators with ArianeSpace sampling matrices. And a Tachytech subquantum inserter? It's the dream system! But no one could ever afford to build the damn thing!"

They emerged into a huge open chamber with enclosed catwalks spiderwebbing the overhead regions. Six squat constructs of shining metal and plastic were arranged in a perfect hexagon, the glassy conduits of the integrators concentrating to the center of the space, merging smoothly into a black, shimmering dome that glittered with ghostly colored lights.

"Oh, it's amazing all right." Pete walked across the room and kicked the black construct, which rang like a huge bell. "It's amazing it hasn't blown up yet. Damn thing just sits here."

"It doesn't work?"

"Doesn't do a damned thing. Hums like crazy, even wiggled a little, but hasn't raised a single millimeter off the ground." The Moor leaned against the subquantum inserter and sighed. "Britt says the elves can figure it out eventually and get us off this rock."

"You don't agree."

He laughed once, a sharp, cynical bark. "I don't think those pointy-eared midgets could find their asses if you gave 'em a map, a mirror, and a strong hint! They aren't qualified to make starships, for Allah's sake!" He pointed at Carl. "But you are. So I found you and brought you here, even though Britt told me not to. So you can fix this piece of junk and get us the hell off this planet before we freeze to death—or get eaten by that lunatic Easter Bunny, whichever comes first."

Carl sighed and rolled up his sleeves.

Carl was buried head-deep in one of the massive integrators, testing control circuits with a pocket oscilloscope, when hands grabbed his ankles and gave a yank. He yelled in alarm and barely managed to keep from taking circuit boards with him as he was hauled bodily from the inspection cavity, into the circle of short, stocky bodies pressed around him.

"Who the hell do you think you are, scab, coming in here and taking work away from rightful union workers?" yelled the person who still had hands around his ankles.

"Huh?" Carl managed, trying to sit up. It finally penetrated into his head that the people around him were elves, pointed ears and all, each carrying some tool like a wrench, spanner or heavy hammer in his small but strong-looking hands. They all looked angry.

"This is a union shop, bucko. You can't just waltz in here and start working without so much as a by-your-leave. We got *rights*," said one of the other elves, who waved a spanner menacingly.

"*Yeah!*" shouted the other elves, "We got rights!" "*Strike!*" "String the scab up!" "Order pizza!"

"Whoa, hey, wait a minute!" yelled Carl, massaging his ankles where the elf had clenched them. The little guy had a grip of steel! "I was asked to come here . . . uh . . . I'm here to help you guys."

"Not by Management. I got a memo. Says you're not authorized." One elf waved a piece of paper. "Says we're the final word here."

Carl grabbed the fluttering paper. It had a stylized candy-cane superimposing a sleigh as a logo. He scanned the paper. It was from Britt Kringle, denying Peter the authority to bring an outside consultant in to work on the starship.

"Ah, I see." He thought for a minute. "Hm. Gentlemen—what union do you belong to?"

The elves looked at each other. The spokesman, the one who had dragged Carl from the engine, stood proudly with his hands on his hips and stated, "Toymakers' Local 101."

"*Toymakers* 101." Carl looked again at the paper, pursed his lips, made tsking sounds. "And are you aware that the *Toymakers* are not now, and has never been, an affiliate of the Brotherhood of Spaceship Riggers and Mechanics, of which I am a *Senior Brother* in good standing?"

The elves looked at him in horror. "Uh . . . " said the spokesman.

"No? Did you even realize that there WAS a Brotherhood of Spaceship Riggers and Mechanics?"

The elves looked sheepish. "Umm . . . er . . . "

"Did you mokes get a waiver from the home office before you started building a starship?" He waited a few seconds, scanned the faces of the crowd, which had started, for some reason, to lose members. "You didn't, did you? A bunch of *toymakers*, building a *spacecraft*, and now you're rousting a *SENIOR BROTHER* engaged in his normal and legal trade, to restrict him on an illegal job? And you try to do it with this patently illegal document, that only proves your complicity in this act of anti-Labor activity?" The spokesman elf blanched, and there were muffled clangs as several elves dropped their tools. Carl could swear there were pops as air slammed into holes as some of the elves vanished from the area.

Carl smiled ever so slightly. "Now, I could just get on the horn and report this to the Head Office. Shut this whole operation down, hit you with so many fines, your Management would be hard pressed to afford a *paperclip!*" moans and cries of terror washed over the tiny knot of elves, "Or we could work this out like . . . well, like true brothers in Labor."

"How?" "What do we need to do?" "Should we order pizza?" Plaintive cries rose from the five, no, four elves.

"I could issue a site waiver . . . " Carl let it hang in the air, eyebrows raised.

The sole remaining elf, the spokesman, looked up at him with pleading eyes. "Could you?"

Carl smiled. "Sure, brother." And reached into his pocket for a pen.

Chapter 6

"Try it now!" yelled Carl, a test probe clamped to a lead, meter held in the other hand. The engines whined into life, a thrumm of power cascading through the entire bulk of the massive vessel like a whirlwind, a torrent of energy that any observer would swear could move a mountain from the sheer sound.

Carl moved the test probe to another lead, then another. He checked readings at three other points. Then he wet his thumb and touched a contact, yelped at the sizzle, put it in his mouth for a moment. "Okay, cut it!" The sound dopplered down, was silent.

Carl crawled down to the engine room floor and checked the computer analysis. "Jervis, did the strain gauges show *anything*?"

The elf shook his head. "No, Carl, nothing. Damn meters were flat on their pins as if glued there. Same thing we've been getting for weeks."

"Grrrahhhhhh!" Carl growled, throwing the meter to the workbench. "That's it. I'm going to take the primary injector apart."

"Carl, we've had it apart three times before you got here. There's nothing wrong with it," Jervis said with a sigh. "We even replaced it with another identical unit. The old unit was used in another ship that lifted twelve days ago. We watched it on the news."

Carl shook his head. "I don't get it. There's no reason why this ship isn't lifting. It's like God doesn't want it to lift."

There was silence in the engine room. The elves, heads lowered, slowly wandered out. Carl kept tinkering with the computer, trying to coax new readings from it. A few minutes later, Black Peter came in and perched on the edge of the workbench.

"Yo, dude," he said. "The elves say you've pronounced it the will of God."

Carl looked up. "Huh? I didn't say that. I mean, I might have said something like that, but it wasn't a pronouncement or anything. It was a metaphor."

Pete sighed. "Trouble is, it isn't anything these people, or I, for that matter, haven't already thought of."

Carl turned off the monitor, swiveled his workstation chair to look at Pete. "You mean folks are actually worried that God might be keeping the ship from lifting?"

Pete nodded. "It's been floated. After all, we're the last. And we're the mythicals, the embodiments of the dreams and myths, fragments of legend and story. Some would say there but for the grace of God we exist at all. Others might say we're corporeal heresy." He stood up. "Come on, let's go get a cup of coffee. It's getting colder in here."

He led Carl to a messroom, drew a cup, handed it to Carl, who took it gratefully. Even aboard the ship, the temperature was starting to drop. The enclave was getting colder too, the powerplant, insulation, and heaters no longer able to keep the intense cold of the freezing planet at bay. Pete pulled up a chair, sat down and wrapped his long, black fingers around his cup. "The rest of the planet has passed Zero Hour. The only thing that's in our favor is that the humidity up here is effectively zero. We've got a few more hours leeway. But, eventually the temp will drop too far even for us. When the carbon dioxide starts falling out of the sky, that'll pretty much be it. We figure that'll happen in about twelve hours. We don't *think* it'll get cold enough for the oxygen to freeze, but none of us will last long enough to find out.

"We've got to figure out what's keeping us from leaving, Carl, or we've had it. Because of me, you'll die with us. And now, it's looking more and more like the Almighty has simply decided to deny us exodus for some reason. If we knew that reason, maybe it is something we could fix, but we don't."

"Fix? What do you mean, fix?"

Pete looked bleak. "Maybe it's one of us He objects to."

Carl looked horrified. "You mean that one of you might have to stay on Earth? A sacrifice?"

Pete nodded. "God may be keeping the ship grounded to keep a heretical idea from leaving the Earth—to keep that idea from going out and getting a second chance on the new worlds." He smiled a wry smile. "Hey, it's not like we're real people, Buddy. We're not. We're like elementals, chunks of Natural force bound into human or human-like shapes by some kind of magic even we don't always understand. Sometimes it's the combined belief of everyone who believed in us . . . sometimes, it's a feedback thing, the strength of the myth itself, feeding back on itself that keeps us going. But the legends change, they mutate over time, the stories change . . .

"Heck, look at fairy tales. The Pied Piper has gone through a dozen mutations. They weren't always happy little stories for entertaining the little brats, you know . . . they were originally stories to terrify, to scare the little shits into obeying. I should know—I was one of those stories. I was a *threat*, the yearly switch in the woodshed that would come and punish the nastiest of the brats so bad they wouldn't *dream* of being bad the next year. I was the universal Yuletide bogey, the blackamoor with the switch that did Santa's dirty work.

"And Cupid—he was a Greek god, shot arrows of love. He wasn't even involved with Valentine's Day until Britt got a hold of him. Saint Valentine was a healer who flauted Roman law by remaining true to his Christian beliefs and was executed for it. The Greeks used to send notes to each other professing their love. Britt got a hold of those stories, blended them, and threw in Cupid as a cute little cherub to tie 'em all together. But people don't dig cute little cherubs these days . . . they're more cynical than that. So the little guy changed.

"He heard Ted Nugent on the radio, and went off on this Great Nuge kick. Followed him all over til the old rocker finally keeled over and died . . . then he watched videos and listened to recorded music. He even went hunting just like his great idol. First time he came back hauling a dead rabbit, the Easter Bunny damn near chewed through the floor, let me tell you.

"Kris is a wreck. You saw the poor guy. He's nothing like he used to be. He used to love giving gifts to the kids. It was in remembrance of the birth of the new God, at Yule, he said, though, as a Moslem, I never really embraced that part. I went with him because he was my friend, and because, as good as he was, he never could bring himself to punish a kid for much of anything. Then Britt got her hooks into him, and Christianized everything . . . and Kris started to get stressed out. The parallel with Bishop Nicholas of Myra, the connections to the birth of Christ, and later, the commercialization beyond all reason. It all weighed heavily on the guy."

Carl nodded. "He seemed hypertensive. Does he have a bad heart?"

Pete looked wan. "I think it's about to break. I don't think it's a bad heart, per se, but he's been through a lot. The world is . . . was . . . a very different place than it was a thousand years ago when we started this sleigh ride. But I think the thing that weighs on him heaviest is the change in Britt."

Carl frowned. "She changed too?"

Pete nodded and sipped his coffee. "I think she changed the most of any of us, even more than that furry maniac Bunny. You would have liked her when she was still mortal. Heck, I even liked her at first, before she married Kris. She was a cute little thing, and full of laughter and joy. She was like a spark of light in the night to Kris, and I didn't blame him a bit for falling ass-over-teakettle for her."

"Were the two of you already immortal by that time?"

"Oh, you betcha! We had been for about a century. Kris was very energetic, and sowing the whole wild oats thing. Everyone paints pictures of him as old and gray, and Mrs. Claus as this little old lady. But at first, they were a pretty randy little couple. But Britt was adamant about one thing: they had to be married first, and it had to be a Christian marriage." He grimaced and gulped his coffee. "That was when things changed. When she married him, she changed. She became like us, immortal, and subject to the same weird laws of our existence. She started to mutate like we do, according to the whims of the mythologies that make us what we are. But she also had that feedback thing I mentioned, and it did weird things to her. She did that whole secular and non-secular thing with Kris, and the Bunny, and Cupid — and she pushed me out. The only thing that kept me from fading away was that some regions of the world still believe in me. Sometimes I think the only thing that kept me alive was a kid's card game given away by an airline." He sighed and looked sad.

Carl drank his coffee. "You said once that she was tapping the economies of Christian countries for money. Tell me more about that."

Pete nodded. "This whole arrangement up here was pretty expensive. We needed money, resources. Kris used to barter for them, but she figured we were more of a public service, a kind of utility that should be publicly funded. And since, in her mind, it was a primarily Christian service, the Christian countries that benefitted from it should pay for it.

"So she used her abilities as a being of legend and an immortal to establish herself in the economic structures of each developing nation and started siphoning off resources. Not a lot at first, but more and more as time went on. When Christmas, Easter, and Valentine's Day became commercial, she started investing in them and double-dipping from the non-secular side of things as well.

"That was when she really diverged. All that economic power really altered her mythological base. She's very different now, kind of a strange mix of Martha Stewart and Bill Gates, with a touch of Billy Graham thrown in for good measure. Kris finds it stressful. I find it frightening. I wish I knew what Allah thinks of it." He frowned into his coffeecup.

A soundless bomb went off behind Carl's eyes. "Oh, shit," he said.

Pete looked up. "What?"

Carl looked at the Moor with terror in his eyes. "I know why the ship doesn't work."

"Why?"

Carl shook his head. "Not here. We need to talk to Kris. And Britt."

Chapter 7

The conference room was frigid, and not entirely because of the temperature. Britt Kringle, Mrs. Claus, sat at the head of the table, glaring knives at Black Peter, who sat at Carl's right hand. Kris Kringle, the corpulent Santa Claus, sat next to his wife, a sphygmomanometer around one chubby wrist.

"I wish to state again, for the record, that I object to this outsider being involved at all in this issue. It goes against my explicit instructions," said Britt, her hands folded tightly on the tabletop before her. Her breath fogged in front of her face. She looked at Carl. "I don't know what you said to my elves, to convince them to work with you, but you won't get away with it. I'm the boss here!"

Kris closed his eyes and looked pained. "Britt, please be quiet."

She whirled and looked at him. "What? You don't mean to give this, this, *mortal* any say over me, do you?"

"I said be *quiet.* If Pete says it's important, I want to hear it." The big man tapped a button on his blood-pressure wristlet, sighed at the readings. "Go ahead, son. Speak your piece."

Carl gulped. "I think I know why the ship doesn't work."

"It will work just fine. The elves will find the problem once you stop obstructing them . . . "

"No," Carl said, "they will not. There is nothing wrong with the ship."

There was silence in the room.

"The ship is in perfect working condition. I will certify that as a professional spaceship technician. That ship should be in space right this minute. It is the most perfect example of spacecraft engineering I have ever seen in my life . . . except that it will not lift off the ground. The question is, what is keeping it from lifting?

"Or, more to the point, WHO?"

Carl looked at Britt Kringle. "I think God is keeping that ship from lifting."

Britt Kringle laughed, a mad look in her eyes. "You're insane. God? Why would He keep our ship from leaving?"

"To keep a horrible crime from being repeated on other worlds, that's why."

Black Pete put a hand on Carl's arm. "Whoa, hey, dude . . . a crime? What crime? I know I mentioned heresy, but like you said, that was a metaphor . . . "

"The crime of genocide. The crime of treason against humanity. The crime of causing the death of Earth."

Everyone's eyes were on him now. "Mrs. Claus, you've been siphoning off resources from Christian nations for centuries, right?"

"Of course I have. Our operation here is expensive."

"Why only the Christian countries?"

"Because our holidays are Christian holidays. Why should non-Christians have to pay for them?"

"Did you siphon funds from the United States?"

She nodded. "Oh, yes. They were one of our largest supporters."

"The United States is not a Christian nation."

"What do you mean? Of course it is!"

"No, it isn't. It has religious freedom. There is no state religion."

"But they celebrate Christmas!"

"Some churches celebrate Christmas as a secular holiday, but it isn't a State holiday. There are Jews in America, and Moslems, and Buddhists, and Wiccans."

"So what? Christmas still affects them. It's a Federal holiday, and they get the benefit of Kris's work . . . "

"So you tap the economy, draw down the budget, drain resources. You cause inflation, unemployment, and shortages that don't exist in countries that don't celebrate Christmas."

"I suppose, yes."

"And this condition exists in other countries that celebrate Christmas?"

"Yes, of course!"

A light started to dawn in Pete's eyes, a horrified, wretched one. His eyes turned from Carl's face to Britt's.

"Mrs. Claus, do you know what causes war?"

"I'm a businesswoman, not a military person. How would I know such things?"

Carl sighed. "The fundamental cause of war, since the beginning of time, is a lack of resources, Mrs. Claus. When one group has resources and another group does not, this causes tension. When that tension goes on long enough, it leads to war . . . and terrorists."

Kris Kringle was now staring at his wife, his face pale.

Carl's voice was soft, gentle. "Mrs. Claus, your campaign of puffing up your husband's so-called holiday, and that of Valentine's Day and Easter, of siphoning off resources from selected nations based on their religion, led to the need for greater industrialization in resource-poor regions. It caused shortages in some areas and surplusses in others that were artificial in nature, based along ideological lines. And because of the religious tensions between nations, the terrorists decided to destroy what they could not control. They crashed asteroids into the parts of Earth that had what they did not, were of religions they did not share." Carl felt as though a a hot brick was sitting in the pit of his stomach. This whole thing stank. But the words had a life of their own.

"Because of you, Earth is dead. You killed it.

"God doesn't want you to leave and do it again somewhere else." Kris Kringle's face clenched in pain, and he grabbed his chest. Black Peter sobbed and put his head on the table.

"No! It isn't true! It can't be!" screamed Britt Kringle. "I've done everything for this world, for my husband!"

Kris Kringle's face unclenched slowly. He looked down at his wife. His pain seemed pain-free for the first time in years. "Britt. Think about it. Were you really doing it for *me*?" He sighed. "Think about what you told Pete a few minutes ago. You told him that *you* were the boss here. Not me. *You.*"

A horrified look swam across Britt's features as her husband's words penetrated her mind. "Kris . . . you don't believe this nonsense, do you?"

The big man waved his hands helplessly. "Love, I don't know what to believe anymore. All I know is, we have friends here that are going to freeze to death very soon unless they get off the planet. If the Creator needs a sign of good faith of some sort, perhaps we should give it."

She looked very strange. "What . . . what are you *saying?*"

He looked sad. "It's very simple. If the Creator is keeping the ship here because of something you have done, then you must, perforce, stay here. And if you stay here, then I will stay with you. If you stay, perhaps the Creator will let the others go and spare their lives."

Britt stood, shaking, and rounded on Black Peter, who was still sitting with his face in his hands. "*You!* This is all *your* doing! Now you've convinced my husband to strand me on a freezing ball of rock so you can go free!" Her face contorted maniacally. "You probably just wanted him to yourself, you little faggoty black *kukkost!*"

Pete sobbed and wrenched his body from the chair. Carl thought he was going to launch himself at the hysterical woman, but the blackamoor swept from the room.

"Mrs. Claus, didn't you hear your husband? He just said that he would be staying here with you," Carl said softly.

"Oh, fuck off, you meddling fool! No one is staying anywhere, least of all on this pathetic mudball!" She began to pace, her face a mask of madness. Her hair began to fly, as if tossed by static. "I'll get the elves back to work. We'll find the flaw in the ship—get it aloft. It *must* fly!" She swept out of the room, heels clicking on the floor like the ticking of a manic clock.

Carl was left in the conference room with Santa Claus. The big man sat quietly in his chair, tears rolling softly down his round cheeks. He looked up at Carl and smiled a sad smile. "I don't blame you, Son," he said softly. "You're right. She's just as mad as the rest of us. Driven that way by the madness of the world around us. Maybe you're wrong about one thing, though. Maybe none of us are meant to leave—because we're too mad." With a sigh, the big man levered himself from the chair and slowly walked from the room.

Carl sat there for a few moments, wondering what to do. Then he heard it.

A chittering sound.

From the air duct.

His hackles rose.

He ran from the room.

Chapter 8

"*Get to work, you lazy bastards!*" screamed Britt Kringle, as she stalked through the atrium. "Get back to that ship and make it work!" No elves came to her call. They sat, dejected, on benches, on chairs, on the catwalks. None moved so much as a hair. "Damn you, do you want to freeze? Get that ship in the sky!"

"They won't work for you anymore, Britt," said a voice behind her. She whirled, and saw the lanky form of Black Peter leaning against a corridor wall, the spoke of the corridor a dark tunnel behind him.

"You black faggot sadist! You've been a thorn in my side for a thousand years! Why can't you just leave me alone? Why can't you just leave Kris alone?" She railed at him, waving her fists.

Pete just looked sad. "Did it ever occur to you that I *can't?* You stupid infidel, I'm not a human being, I'm a bundle of mythology in a chimneysweep's outfit! Do you think I make up my own rules? And, for your information, I'm no more a *kwanii*, a faggot, than you are. I like girls just fine, thank you, not that you ever bothered to ask. I hang around Kris because he's my best friend, and because, once we became legendary immortals, *I couldn't leave him anymore!* My myth depends on his, just like his depends on mine! The legend of *Schwartzer Peter* doesn't *exist* except in connection with Santa Claus, you *antareh gav*, annoying cow! You want me to leave, get all those Germans and Poles and Russians and Norwegians to stop believing in me, and I'll fade away like a bad dream.

"But given any choice in the matter, I wouldn't leave him no matter what you said. He's my best friend, and I love him. Not in the way you think, but because he's my *friend*, and he needs me." With that, Pete turned and started walking away.

"Don't you walk away from me like that! I need help getting this ship in the air!"

"It won't happen. You can't get it to fly. You can't leave the planet."

She snorted. "You don't believe that space-mech's nonsense about me causing the death of the Earth, do you?"

Pete paused. "Yes," he said, simply. He walked away down the corridor.

"It isn't my fault!" Britt shouted at his retreating back. "We needed the resources! The Christian countries *owed* us, it was ours by right! Then those greeting card companies were just raking in bucks, and the toy companies. They were cashing in on Kris, and we were getting *snabel*. I couldn't let THAT go on, could I? And movies—the movies alone—I had to, Peter! I didn't have any choice!" A wrench dropped by her feet, startling her. She jumped to the side. "It wasn't my fault when Constantinople was sacked. That was just a vicious rumor." A hammer dropped behind her, clanging on the deck. She danced away from the sound. "I didn't have anything to do with the death of Nicholas of Myra! It wasn't me! And I didn't have anything to do with the assassination of Archduke Ferdinand!" A spanner spun from the darkness and nicked her shin. "And Kennedy would have been killed eventually, by someone. It wasn't my fault!" A rain of tools fell from the catwalks, clattered all around her. "And I'm sorry I slept with that President! He said he'd get Bin Laden off our backs!" She ran from the atrium, tears streaming from her eyes.

She ran around corners, into a maze of hazy corridors, clouded by tears. She heard a strange chittering sound, a cold, chilling sound that she knew she should recognize, but her heart didn't want to grasp . . .

" . . . can't let them *get* me, Missy Ma'am . . . " hissed the voice off to her left.

And the teeth slashed into her leg.

Chapter 9

Carl crawled into through the inspection grating and sighed, hauling out his test meter. He clipped the ground probe to the frame and started checking circuits, thinking about the Bunny chasing Mrs. Claus through the corridors of the complex. He shuddered convulsively.

Was he right? He wasn't sure anymore. It sounded right, but there was something nagging at him, something he had missed . . .

"It's not your fault, Carl," said a voice. Carl started and banged his head on the low ceiling of the access shaft.

"Kris?" His voice echoed in the confined metal shaft.

"Yes, son. I wanted to chat at you a bit, and I saw you come in her. Do you mind if I chat a bit at you while you work?"

Carl laid his forehead on the cool metal of the shaft wall. He felt as if he had failed the jolly fat man. He had found something, yes, but it was something horrible, something terrible about the man's own wife.

Sigh. "Of course not, Kris."

He pried a cover off a control module and began testing branch circuits, reading off the values on his meter. Everything checked out perfectly. Exactly as it should be. Exactly as it always was, in every starship engine he had ever worked on. So why didn't the damn thing work?

"Things weren't always so grim, Carl. Things just changed. They always just seemed to change out from under me. I never used to be so damned fat, you know. I was a slender lad when I was young. That's

what caught Britt's eye. I cut a dashing figure in a fur suit back
then . . . "

The probe fell from Carl's fingers and hit him in the forehead. He
lay there, staring at the module. He squirmed, and pulled the cover off
another module, stared at it. He pulled off another cover, stared at *that.*

"But then this artist fellow did some new pictures of me after reading that 'Night Before Christmas' poem . . . they were beautiful, don't
get me wrong . . . but he did 76 damn engravings of me as downright
corpulent! And old! Dammit, I found myself wheezing when I walked
down a corridor, and my beard went white practically overnight! The
kiddies loved it . . . but Britt just seemed more distant than ever. She
just got colder, somehow . . . "

They were all perfectly normal. That was what was wrong. They
were all absolutely normal. One-hundred-percent perfectly fragging
normal. So normal they *stank.*

"I tried to think if it was anything I had done, anything I had said . . .
but Carl, it wasn't anything. It was just that damn artist fellow. One day
I was virile and thin and could wrestle a sea lion . . . and the next, Britt
was feeding me Geritol and asking if I should really eat that cookie . . .
and there suddenly all these Christmas cards with these new pictures
of me, and Britt was so distant, so cold." The jolly old elf gave a deep,
sad sigh that echoed in the corridors of the dead starship.

Carl stopped what he was doing at the sound of that sigh. *Christmas cards.* "Oh, shit," Carl said, laying an arm across his eyes, realizing
the depth of his mistake. He had presence of mind enough to push
the covers back on the modules before he squirmed back out of the
inspection tube.

He had to find Peter. Fast.

Santa watched the retreating back of the starship mech as he ran
from the open airlock.

"Gee, lad . . . was it something I said?" The big man just sat there
dejectedly. "Now what was that dratted artist's *name?* Mann . . . no . . .
Mast! Thomas Mast . . . what a naughty boy *he* was . . . "

He found the Moor in the conference room, a long stick of supple
wood on the table before him. The radio on the table next to the
willow switch hummed faintly, and Carl recognized the sound of Cupid's
wings coming through the speaker.

"Peter, I need to talk to you," he said.

Peter waved him off. "Not right now, man . . . we need to find that crazy lepus before he munches the Old Lady."

"But this is important!"

Peter cocked an eye on him. "Like keeping a woman from being eaten by a fertility demon isn't? Look, Carl, that was a nice piece of detective work . . . but we've done this before. Give us half an hour, tops, and I'll get back to you."

Carl took a deep breath. "Mrs. Claus didn't kill the Earth." Peter looked directly at him.

"Say what?"

"That isn't why the ship doesn't work."

"I thought you said . . ."

"I was wrong."

"Aw, *crap* . . . Carl . . ."

"Hey, look . . . I just figured it out, okay? This place has had me all screwed up. It took me a while to get my bearings!"

Peter sighed. "Okay. You have my attention. What's the real answer."

"You guys aren't gods."

"I could've told you *that.*"

"But I've been reacting to you as if you *were*! But you're not. You're *legends*. You don't create a damn thing! You *react* to the world, you don't *make* it! When the world changes, you change to match. You don't alter the world to suit *you*!" He pointed out the glass wall of the conference room at the starship. "Your ship, for example. Here we've got a work of technical art by a bunch of elves and toymakers . . . but do they tinker with it? Yeah, the corridors are pretty . . . but do they innovate even so much as a single circuit? NO! *Every single wire is off the shelf!*

"Every one of you has mutated to match an image of the world around you, regardless of how you might feel about it. Hell, even you are stuck to Kris like a limpet mine when you would probably rather not watch him self-destruct, and probably rather not listen to his wife run you down all the time and shoot lasers at you! But you can't leave because you don't act, you *react.*

"Mrs. Claus couldn't have killed the Earth. She couldn't have instigated the changes that caused the political stresses. She simply reacted to them when they happened on their own."

Peter's face changed to a mask of stark terror. "Damn, Carl . . . that makes *sense*. But why are we stuck here, then? What does God want from us?"

"I think I got that part right. I think he wants someone to stay behind. I just think I got the *reason* wrong."

Chapter 10

"OW! Damn you, you furry pest!" Britt screeched, grabbing the Bunny by the scruff of his neck. He squealed as she yanked his teeth from her ankle and shook him like a baby's rattle. "What the hell do you think you're doing?"

"God won't let ship leave until you die," the miserable creature whined, his whiskers bright with her blood. "I *gotta* go, Missy!"

Britt sighed. "I know, you crazy little furball. I know. But not because of the reason that asshole starship mech thinks. He's wrong, you know."

The Bunny squirmed in her grip. "But what if he's right, Missy? What if you *did* kill the world?"

She snorted. "Come on, you stupid creature, think! When was the last time any of us could actually change anything on our own? That idiot got it backwards! It took me a while to get over the shock and figure it out, but the fool got the cart before the horse!"

The little creature stopped squirming. "Wait . . . I think I see . . . we don't change things . . . we are changed!"

"That's my little carrot-muncher! So what is needed isn't so much for one of us to be punished as for one of us to *change*, to change to match this new Earth, this new situation, just like we always do."

The Bunny nodded. "Old God dies with winter. New God brings Spring!" Britt looked confused. "Makes sense! Listen! Winter comes with death of old God. At Spring festival, new God celebrates coming of Spring and thawing ground for new planting."

Britt shook her head, not comprehending.

"Don't you see, Missy? You must go into Earth, be like Old God. Be reborn like New God in Spring when Earth thaws!" The Bunny nodded brightly. "I remember the old ways. I was a symbol of Spring. I can help." He described what was necessary.

Britt listened. When the Bunny was done, she was silent for a moment. Then she whispered: "I guess I'm going to take my husband's religion after all."

Pete followed the sound of singing, a long, slender wooden rod clenched in his hands. He raised the commlink to his mouth. "Cupe, you got anything?"

"Got footprints, hers. Goes into the steam tunnel in sector three."

Pete swore. "*Nikomak!* I'll meet you there." He ducked through an inspection hatch, swung his lanky frame down a ladder into a narrow passageway. The walls were beaded with condensation. The sounds had stopped several minutes ago, and that chilled him more than the sounds had.

"*Great Nuge . . .* " came a tinny whisper from the commlink. He snatched at the device. "What?"

"Get to corridor A-24, intersection J-4," said the cherub.

Peter accelerated to a trot. He reached the specified location a moment later, and found Cupid, bending over something on the floor. He looked over the cherub's wing, and his eyes bugged out. A little, fuzzy lump lay in the center of a large chalked pentagram on the green tile floor. The pentagram had been drawn around a tall metal stanchion. The stanchion was wrapped with festoons of ribbon . . . at closer inspection, it was brightly-colored ribbon cable from a nearby electronics locker.

The floor, the pentagram, and the stanchion were all glowing bright gold. The Bunny was bathed in light, his fur shiny and sleek. He looked as if he were asleep.

"Is he asleep?"

"Yup."

"He hasn't looked that cute in fifty years."

"Shit, man, I think he's cured."

Pete pulled out a syringe and a canvas sack. "Let's not take chances," Then he leaned over, injected the sleeping Bunny, and gently placed him in the sack.

He felt a murmur of power through him as the golden light touched him. It felt warm. It felt like . . . like something he hadn't felt in a long, long time. He reached out and touched the glowing floor . . .

. . . He was standing on a grassy field, a tall pole of golden wood before him. The wood was draped with ribbons of silk of a dozen colors, and a golden-haired woman sat against it, her hair garlanded with flowers.

"Hello, Black Peter," she said. "I've been expecting you."

Black Peter looked at the power of his friend's wife and sighed. "Hello, Britt."

"I'll take good care of Earth. After a time, she'll thaw out nicely, and people will be able to live here again. That's what God wanted all along—someone to stay and defrost the freezer. The ship will be able to leave now. You take good care of Kris, you infidel bastard!"

Peter couldn't speak. He just nodded.

EPILOGUE

Carl tapped the last commands into the sequencer. The hooter went off, and motors rumbled as the big dome over the atrium rolled back. The span of gleaming white ice that remained flared into vapor a moment later as sixteen huge lasers blazed, throwing the entire output of the city's powerplant against it. Then the cold, cold blue sky shone overhead. The first few flakes of dry ice snow were starting to fall just a few miles north. They had cut it close, almost too close.

"Everyone belted in?" Carl said. Jervis nodded and gave him a thumbs up.

"All departments show green lights. Everyone's all nestled down snug in their beds. Even Noggin and his reindeer are tucked in tight."

"Ready, Pete?" Carl said to the blackamoor in the control chair next to him.

The lanky black man sighed. "Yeah, light this candle."

Kris Kringle, a new . . . or perhaps a very old twinkle in his eye, spoke from the other control chair. "Yes, light this candle."

Carl tapped the execute tab.

The starship throbbed with hope, and the last legends of Earth lifted into the cerulean sky.

The End